JEWEL STICKER STORIES

The Magic Carpet Ride

By Jennifer Dussling

Illustrated by Jerry Smath

For Jessica Dubin—J.S.

GROSSET & DUNLAP · NEW YORK

Ali was walking through the city when he saw a group of people by the Sultan's palace. What was going on? A royal announcement had just been posted. He went over to read it.

A birthday party for the princess! Ali wanted to go. But he would have to give the princess a present.

The sun was just setting. Ali had plenty of time to find a present by morning. He lit a lantern, whistled to his pet bird, and unrolled a carpet. It was a rare magic carpet. He got on, and it slowly rose off the ground. It hovered in the air for a moment. Then the magic carpet zoomed up and away!

Put a jewel sticker on Ali's lamp.

The magic carpet soared over the city and past the Sultan's palace. Ali spotted the princess leaning out her window, looking at the stars. She didn't seem at all like a princess. She seemed like someone Ali might have as a friend. He had to find her a very special present!

Make the biggest star glow with a jewel sticker.

Ali headed the carpet toward the marketplace. Finding a present here would be easy. But he flew by every last table, and nothing was quite right.

Put a jewel sticker on your favorite thing in the marketplace.

The magic carpet flew out of the city and over
the desert. Suddenly, palm trees loomed up from the
miles and miles of sand. Ali rubbed his eyes. Could it
be? Yes! It was an oasis in the middle of the desert!
Ali stopped for a drink of cool water.

Do you see the moon reflected in the water?
Give it extra glow with a jewel sticker.

The magic carpet passed over a long merchant caravan. Colorful silk tents were set up for the night, and all the traders' camels were staked outside.

Ali pulled the carpet to a stop. "I'll see if these merchants have a present fit for the princess." He looked at dresses and jewels, bottles and baskets, but nothing caught his eye.

Make the caravan torches glow with jewel stickers.

In the side of a desert dune, Ali saw a dark opening. "I wonder what's in there," he said. He went inside and what did he find? A cave full of marvelous treasure—and a huge sleeping genie! Ali knew he definitely didn't want to wake him. "Let's get out of here," he whispered to the carpet.

Put a jewel sticker on the genie.

Ali yawned. He had been flying around all night and still hadn't found a present. Where else could he look?

Ali headed to the royal zoo on the carpet. There were golden tigers, noble elephants, and fancy Arabian horses. "What can I give the princess that she doesn't already have?" he sighed.

Put a sticker on the tiger's collar.

At dawn, Ali flew tiredly back to the Sultan's palace—
without a present. He watched the long line of rich sheiks
carrying all sorts of expensive gifts. It had been silly to think
that the princess would ever want a present from someone
like him.

Ali was just about to go home when he remembered
the princess leaning out her window, looking at the sky.
Suddenly he knew exactly what he could give her!

Put a jewel sticker on your favorite gift.

Ali flew over the heads of the rich sheiks and into the palace throne room. When the princess saw Ali and the magic carpet, she jumped up from her pillow.

"I know my gift isn't gold or jewels, Princess, but would you like to go on a magic carpet ride?" Ali asked.

The princess laughed. "I'd love to!" she said.

Decorate the princess's crown
with a jewel sticker.

Ali stayed for the entire party. Then when it was finally over, the princess and Ali went for a magic carpet ride above the rooftops of the city.

"The stars are so much brighter up here," the princess said to Ali. "This was the best present of all!"

Make the city and the stars sparkle and glow with your jewel stickers!

The next morning, everyone in the city was just
waking up. But where was Ali?
In a corner, under the magic carpet, fast asleep.